Miss Mopp's Lucky Day

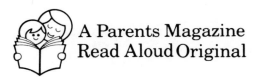

A Parents Magazine
Read Aloud Original

Library of Congress Cataloging in Publication Data
McGuire, Leslie. Miss Mopp's lucky day.
SUMMARY: Because it looks like rain and Miss Mopp
remembers something she forgot, disaster is
diverted on her trip through the woods.
[1. Luck — Fiction] I. Silver, Jody. II. Title
PZ7.M4462Mi [E] 81-4879
ISBN 0-8193-1061-1 AACR2
ISBN 0-8193-1062-X (lib. bdg.)

Miss Mopp's Lucky Day

By LESLIE McGUIRE   Pictures by JODY SILVER

Parents Magazine Press • New York

To David: May all your days be lucky — L.M.

To my daughter, Leigh — J.S.

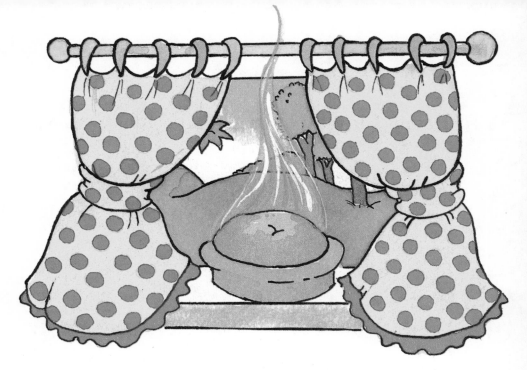

Miss Mopp was the best baker in town.
She baked all kinds of cakes —
pink cakes and yellow cakes,
big cakes and small cakes,
plain cakes and fancy cakes.

One morning Miss Mopp
woke up and said,
"Today is my lucky day!
I just know I will sell
all my cakes."

So, as soon as she finished her baking,
Miss Mopp got dressed and
carefully wrapped her cakes
to take to town.

Just as she stepped outside,
the sun went behind a cloud.
It was a big, gray rain cloud.
But Miss Mopp did not see it.

She went a few steps, then stopped.
"Did I forget something?"
she asked herself.
"Oh well, I can't think what it might be."
And on she went.

TO
TOWN

As she walked, the smell of
the delicious cakes went before her.
It was a very good smell.

Now, deep in the woods,
smelling that smell,
was a bear.
"Mmm," said the bear.
"Miss Mopp's cakes.
I want to gobble them up!"
And the bear hid behind a tree.

The bear was not the only one
smelling the smell of Miss Mopp's cakes.
There was also a moose.
"Mmm," said the moose.
"Miss Mopp's cakes.
I want to gobble them up!"
So the moose hid
on the other side of the tree.

Miss Mopp walked along happily.
She did not see that up in the tree,
smelling the smell of her delicious cakes,
there was a bird.
"Mmm," said the bird.
"Miss Mopp's cakes.
I want to gobble them up!"
And the bird hid behind a big leaf.

The sky was getting
darker and darker.
Miss Mopp tried to remember
what she had forgotten.
She still did not see
the big, gray rain cloud.

And she did not see the fat raccoon
and the furry rabbit.
They were smelling the smell
of the delicious cakes, too.
"Mmm," they each said.
"Miss Mopp's cakes.
I want to gobble them up!"
And they hid in two hollows in the tree.

Then, just as the bear, the moose,
the bird, the raccoon, and the rabbit
were about to jump out
to gobble up the cakes,
Miss Mopp stopped and yelled...

"MY UMBRELLA!
I forgot my UMBRELLA!"
And she ran back to her house while...

The rabbit dashed out
  and hit the raccoon
    who tripped the bear
      who fell on the moose
        who got hit on the head by the bird.

Miss Mopp made it back to her house
just before the rain began.
She picked up her umbrella
and started off again.

She walked through the woods,
past the tree, and into town,
without meeting anyone at all.

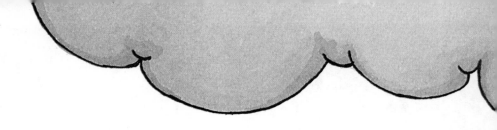

When she got to the bake shop
she saw a line outside.
"My stars!" said Miss Mopp.
"Look at all
those customers
waiting to buy
my cakes.
This is truly
my lucky day!"

But Miss Mopp
didn't know how lucky
she really was, did she?

ABOUT THE AUTHOR

LESLIE MCGUIRE believes people are lucky if they *think* they are lucky. For example, if Miss Mopp was feeling gloomy, she might have said, "My stars, what a dreadful day! I forgot my umbrella, I had to run back home for it, then it rained and my cakes were almost ruined!" "So you see," explains Ms. McGuire, "it's all in how you look at it!"

Ms. McGuire was a teacher and a children's book editor before she turned to writing children's books full time. Her first book for Parents, which she wrote and illustrated, was *This Farm is a Mess*.

Ms. McGuire lives in New York City with her husband and their five year old son. She thinks they have lots of lucky days. "I hope all *your* days are lucky, too!" she says.

ABOUT THE ARTIST

JODY SILVER says she liked Miss Mopp immediately, even though she and Miss Mopp don't have much in common. "For example, I can't cook at all," she says. "Even my two cats don't like my cooking. I think they prefer Purina!"

Ms. Silver writes and illustrates children's books and she is also an animator. An animator is a person who draws the pictures for cartoons, like the ones you see on television. Ms. Silver has animated cartoons for *Sesame Street,* and she has made two animated films of her own. *Miss Mopp's Lucky Day* is the first book she has illustrated for Parents.

Ms. Silver lives in New York City with her husband and their daughter.